Alphas of the Waterworld
Book 6

STOLEN BY THE SUBMARINE

USA TODAY BESTSELLING AUTHOR

V.T. BONDS

Go to https://vtbonds.com for a complete list of books by V.T. Bonds.

For new releases, discounts, and Knotty Exclusives, subscribe to V.T. Bonds' newsletter at

https://vtbonds.com/newslettersubscriber.

This Dark Omegaverse Romance is knot for the faint of heart. If explicit scenes, OTT possessive alphas, violence, and D/s themes offend you, please abstain.

I made my alpha reader cry. Oops.

She also said,

"Holy shit balls!!!! What have you done? BOW DOWN TO THE DAMN QUEEN..."

So... take that however you want...

CONTENTS

ALPHAS OF THE WATERWORLD

Series Introduction

They ate the women first.

Back when the rains drowned the crops and turned the earth into a polluted swamp, men on the verge of starvation preyed upon the weak. Urged on by *The Madness*—a combination of infectious mold, hunger, and desperation—they murdered and consumed the women and children until the population dwindled.

Faced with extinction, humanity used *The Madness* to evolve. Dynamics emerged, fracturing humanity into three subspecies: alphas, betas, and omegas.

It should have worked. The race should have thrived.

Alphas had the brawn and fortitude to protect their own. Betas had the wisdom and skills needed to rebuild. Omegas had the endurance to accept the alpha's attentions, as well as a biological need to nurture their offspring.

But human nature proved itself to be broken.

Greed pushed alphas to war. Fear made betas cower. Abuse turned omegas barren.

As the rains continued, the land became lost amidst the seafloor. Continents disappeared. Water reigned. The sky slowly ceased its weeping.

Massive floating cities emerged, forged from buoyant ruins, battle-wrecked ships, and upended buildings. Survivors added piles of wreckage to the crafts until a mishmash of rusty metal and concrete provided enough space for pockets of civilization to form.

Dirt replaced gold in value. The alphas hoarded every granule and pillaged the wreckage until they owned every viable seed on the now-oceanic planet.

Except the seeds refused to grow, just as the omegas refused to breed.

The alphas were strong, but the omegas possessed all the power.

Chaos ruled the Waterworld.

CHAPTER 1

Coral

I curl my toes out of the reach of the grimy, seeking fingers and tighten my grip on the bars above me for better balance as I avoid the arms reaching through my cage. After hours of maintaining my awkward pose, my entire body aches, but I ignore my burning muscles and tingling fingers and focus on the dark thunderclouds gathering on the horizon. Although the sea looks calm near the boat, white-capped waves crash in the distance.

The sun beats down on the tarp stretched over the top of my cage. My knuckles brush against the rough material as it flaps in the hot breeze. Even in the shade, my pale skin throbs as though on the verge of sunburn. The scent of fear, alpha aggression, and death clogs my sinuses.

Sweat runs down my sides, plastering my skimpy dress to my skin. Barely long enough to reach my upper thighs, the thin material offers little protection from the sun and even less from the crowd's leering eyes. My skin crawls as fingers inch closer to my legs. If my cage weren't on a pedestal, I'd have no way to avoid the crazed alphas' hands.

I shift my gaze to the small gathering of people on the upper deck, but avert my eyes when fear skitters down my spine.

The Head Sister, who leads an organization of beta females so expansive yet secretive no one knows their true numbers, watches the proceedings with calculating eyes. Even without direct eye contact, her disapproval spears into my chest.

The bruise around my ankle throbs. I didn't move fast enough earlier, and a man grabbed me. She'll never forgive me, which means I'll feel her wrath after she sells my first heat.

Her instructions were clear: remain untouched and unmarred to bring the highest price.

I failed.

Tears sting the back of my eyes.

Even though my soul aches from loneliness, I hold no hope of filling the void. The Sisters may sell my body time and time again, but the disgusting men swarming the cage solidify what they've told me my entire life: I will not survive underneath an alpha without their protection.

Alphas are too self-centered. Too brutal. Too animalistic.

At least with The Sisters looking over me, I won't die a gruesome death.

I wish the storm would roll in faster.

The pile of dead bodies underneath my cage grows as the crazed, half-starved alphas fight over the chance to reach through the bars. At least the wind and rain of a storm would wash away the worst of the smell.

I don't want to do this anymore. Nausea grips me as fingertips graze my heel.

The ship jerks. Vibrations well up from the bowels of the ship. Violent, white-capped waves smash against the hull on the port side.

Untethered cages topple and slide against the floorboards. Bodies fly. Snarls and screams batter my eardrums.

My knees bash against the side of the cage, but I keep hold of the top bars as the deck swings in the opposite direction.

A hand wraps around my calf. I kick at their elbow, but the man refuses to let go even as the ship changes direction and he smacks face first into the bars. Blood pours from his nose, and I jam my heel between his eyes on instinct.

He releases me. I clench my fingers tighter and walk my feet up the bars to brace myself in the top corner, but a jarring crash nearly sends me flying across my cage. The crunch of metal on metal encourages a louder, more desperate cry from the crowd.

I fight nausea as the deck pitches impossibly further to the starboard side. The pile of bodies under my cage shifts, pulling those standing on top along the deck with them.

Hissing pulls my attention to the sea beyond the hull.

A gigantic black beast rises from the depths of the ocean. Easily twice the size of the slave market ship, the metal monstrosity continues to grow as it cuts through the hull, locking both vessels together with wrenching finality.

When the sharp nose of the beast reaches the main deck, it stops its ascent with another eerie hiss of air.

Even through the screaming and chaos, my ears pick out the creaking of the pedestal underneath my cage.

A scream burns my throat as I freefall. Trapped in my cage, I slam against the bars as it topples over. The cracking of bones and squishing of organs releases the meal The Sisters gave me before the auction.

With the bars digging into my shins and my knuckles still white around the steel bars of the ceiling, I kneel and vomit into the tangle of limbs trapped under my cage as it lies on its side. My arms shake, but I can't force my fingers to let go.

Despite the horror of my predicament, a deeper sense of dread settles into my chest. With premonition jangling through my veins, I lift my head and look over my shoulder.

A circular hatch opens on the top of the black beast and the broadest shoulders in existence rise from the depths. Too large to pass through with ease, the alpha maneuvers himself out with predatory grace.

My stomach clenches as our eyes meet.

Amber orbs fill my vision. The world narrows. Nothing will save me from this male.

With lethal calm, he pulls first one, then another, blade from his thigh holsters. Covered in tight black material, he makes the simple t-shirt and pants ensemble look deadly and mysterious, like a warrior from before the rains began. His black boots glimmer in the sunlight as he stalks down the nose of his ship.

Movement from behind him breaks my trance. Man after man emerges from the belly of the submarine.

A snarl sounds above my head. I jerk toward the opposite side of my cage, narrowly avoiding the crazed alpha's fingers as he reaches through the bars.

Madness resumes. Bodies block out the sun as those too lost to instinct swarm my fallen cage. I scream, kick, and fight with all my might, but there's no escape for me.

A low growl steals the breath from my lungs. I curl into a ball on my side, ignoring the hands tugging at my limbs.

Sunlight heats the side of my face. I glance up as massive hands curl around the shoulders of the man directly above me and yank him away. With a sickening crunch, the amber-eyed alpha breaks the male's neck and tosses him aside.

My insides clench and wicked heat pulses through my veins.

I must be in shock. This cannot be real. It's only an estrous-induced nightmare.

Nails dig into my flesh and wrench my arm away from my leg. I twist my wrist and lash out, kicking my attacker in the face and snapping his elbow in the wrong direction. With his arm trapped between the bars, he screams in my face until hands wrap around his throat from behind.

He disappears.

My savior systematically destroys the males swarming my cage. His snarl as he warns one of his men away clenches something deep within my abdomen.

He won't share the glory.

Maybe he won't share the spoils, either?

Eerie silence descends. I peek through the curtain of my hair.

Unlike the blown pupils of the crazed males, *The Submarine* stares down at me with sparkling amber orbs.

My nipples harden and lust pulses between my legs, but the stench and horror of my surroundings ground me in the present. I tremble as scarred knuckles wrap around the bars of my cage.

With terrifying ease, he yanks open the door, rips it off its hinges, and tosses the metal aside. My heart leaps and fear locks me in place as he reaches into my cage.

He wraps unyielding fingers around my biceps. My skin ignites. I jolt in shock.

Instinct swallows me whole. I sink into the feral animal lurking within my soul. Biting, scratching, and hissing, I fight with shocking intensity, but my strength is no match for the massive alpha.

He captures my wrists, pins them to the small of my back in one of his gigantic hands, and plasters our fronts together. I hiss as he yanks my head back by my hair.

The world drops out from under my feet. Specks of gold shine from the ring of amber around his enlarged pupils. His nostrils flare and the most delicious vibration leaks from his chest.

I'm helpless against his purr. My bones melt as it resonates throughout my entire body.

"I found you, little omega. You're mine now."

His deep timbre reaches into my soul and awakens instinctual needs.

I shake my head as much as his grip will allow.

A devilish smirk tilts his lips, creasing the thin white scar trailing from the corner of his nose down to his chin. He pulls my head further back, exposing my neck, and shifts our fronts together, rubbing my hard nipples against his impossibly harder abdominals.

My breath hitches as he leans down and nuzzles my temple. Goosebumps pepper my flesh as his breath ghosts over the sensitive shell of my ear.

"Fight me all you want, angel. Nothing will stop me from dragging you into my hell."

Despite the grime covering me from head to toe and the cloying stench of death wafting from the piles of bodies lying around us, his alpha pheromones invade my nostrils and short-circuits my mind.

A switch flips in my brain. My higher thoughts leap out of reach. I snarl.

Pure delight sparks in his amber orbs.
I’m doomed.

CHAPTER 2

Port

She's ethereal perfection. White hair. Pale skin. Expressive grey eyes. Full lips. Fuller hips. Narrow waist. High, pert breasts.

If I were a nicer male, I'd thank whoever took such great care of her, but possessive jealousy spears through me.

Too close to losing control, I toss her over my shoulder and enjoy her struggles as I retrace my steps. My boots splash in the pools of blood covering the deck. Bodies with slit throats, caved in chests, and missing limbs litter the path, but I traverse my back trail with ease and use the broken railing to step onto the battering ram of my submarine.

Tiny fists thump against my back. Her feminine snarls arrow straight to my balls.

I quicken my pace and wrap my hand around the back of her thigh. She snarls and sinks her nails into my lower back.

"That's it, baby. Draw blood. I'll enjoy returning the favor," I rumble through a throat thick with desire.

She stiffens. I take advantage, pull her off my shoulder, and encase her in my arms before jumping through the open hatch. My shoulders graze the lip, but the pain is worth it as I protect my omega from unnecessary harm and land on my feet.

I step into the darkness, not needing the harsh light of the sun to know which direction to head. The female wriggles in my arms. I tighten my grip on her. She kicks my shins with her bare feet.

Unwilling to deal with broken toes, I snarl and force her legs around my hips. Her sound of distress travels down my spine and pulses through my hard shaft. I brace my forearm under her ass and yank her head back by her hair.

Her light grey orbs reflect the scant light. I stop in front of the watertight door and use my body to block my men's view of her as they descend the ladder. They wisely avoid touching me as they pack into the chamber. The last man swings the hatch closed. Metal squeaks as he turns the hand wheel and locks us away from the world.

Lust roars through me as the tiny, delicate body plastered to mine trembles. The heat of her pussy scorches the front of my pants. I curse the fabric and the length of my shaft as it lies trapped against my leg instead of running through her folds. I wish for a smaller cock for the first time in my life.

Sanity returns. Red light bathes us.

A wet spot forms on the leg of my trousers as liquid need escapes my tip. My knot bulges, making the confines of my pants even more uncomfortable.

Unable to resist, I grind my hips into hers. She whimpers.

I snarl and press her against the door. She gasps. My faithful men shuffle further away, but their pheromones piss off the possessive alpha beast raging within my soul.

The ship shudders, but I barely register the vibrations through the shaking of my soul as I sink my tongue into my angel's open mouth. Her nails pierce my chest. She tries to turn her face away.

I growl and stroke my tongue over hers. The warm, wet heat of her mouth entrances me as her sweetness explodes along my tastebuds, and I dominate every inch of her depths with sensual licks. When I pull back and nip her bottom lip, she hiccups and shakes her head.

I drop my forehead to hers and force myself to speak through the haze of lust.

"Beg me. Worship me. Curse me. It's all the same down here in my hell, angel."

She shakes her head harder. I snarl and tighten my fist in her hair.

"No matter how hard you fight or how loud you scream, no one can help you now. You're mine," I promise.

"I don't want to die," she whispers.

I lick the shell of her ear despite the filth covering her, so addicted to her taste I'll do anything for more, and moan.

"You won't. Not for a long, long time. I plan to enjoy your body for years. I'll have you trapped on my knot and full of my seed for decades. I can't wait to watch your belly swell with my offspring."

Her pupils shrink. The light blinks, offering me red snapshots of her response. Shock parts her swollen lips. Yearning fills her face.

Disbelief closes her expression.

Anger rumbles from my chest.

I will own every piece of her. She'll see. I'll make her regret doubting me.

I've searched for an omega for over a decade, and plan to enjoy her for much longer. Every time we surface near another vessel, we risk our lives, not only because we expose ourselves to the diseases of the outside world, but also because we garner attention from power hungry alphas.

The ocean may isolate the overpopulated cities, but news travels fast over the open waters. Resource deprived pockets of civilization would do anything to ruin my underwater empire.

She wriggles against me, letting me know I'm squishing her too hard against the door.

"Want to make a deal with the devil, little angel?" I whisper against her temple.

She shakes her head.

I chuckle and nip her ear.

"I've never been allowed to make deals. The Sisters are always in charge."

Something in her tone reaches deep into my chest and squeezes the dilapidated organ pumping within. The sensation is almost strong enough to override the jealousy roaring through me. Almost.

I snarl and take her mouth with my own, finding the perfect outlet for my anger in her soft, wet heat. She avoids my advances, but I grind my hips against hers and demand she accept me.

At the first tentative flick of her tongue, my knot balloons and tests the seams of my trousers. Fresh wetness seeps from my tip. I release her hair and splay my fingers over the back of her head to protect her from the metal door as I delve deeper into her mouth. With my other arm bracing her ass, I flex my fingers into the back of her thigh, enjoying the softness of her flesh as her dress rides impossibly higher.

Her small sound of delight has me reaching to free my cock, but the labored breaths of the men behind me snap my attention away from my omega.

I snarl and wrench my mouth away from hers, but stay close so her breath washes over my lips as I gather myself.

"I'm the one in control of your future now, little female. No one else."

A shiver wracks her from head to toe. Someone shifts behind me.

It's too much.

I pin the side of her face against my chest and step away from the door before releasing her head just long enough to twist the lever and stalk into the hall.

Like the devil himself, I'll take this fallen angel and make her mine. I'll rut, knot, and ruin her until she swells with my child and gives me the only thing missing in my sunken oasis.

The future.

CHAPTER 3

Coral

I cling to his shirt, afraid of falling into the abyss as he weaves through the maze of metal. Too tall and broad to walk upright in the narrow hall, he leans forward and angles his hips, and when my head finally stops spinning, I realize he does so to prevent me from bashing my knees into the walls.

Without me in his arms, he wouldn't have to stoop so low, but he moves with such grace I take far longer than I normally would to notice.

He steals a sliver of my omega heart with his small display of care.

The Sisters always warned me against alpha brutality, but they never mentioned the potency of alpha kindness.

I have no defenses against him. Violence would be easier to handle.

With his massive hand holding my head to his chest, his muscular arm blocks most of my view, but flashes of red light reveal well-kept, painted walls and legible signs. The steady beat of his heart against my ear tempts me to nuzzle into him, but with only his shirt between my sex and his abdominals, I'm too aware of my predicament.

Despite the terror flowing through my veins, his promise to use me for years comforts me, even though a large part of me doesn't believe him.

My entire life, I've only seen and heard stories of alphas using their strength for violence. The crazed men swarming my cage represent my expectations.

Maybe it's because I've spent years hardening my heart against what The Sisters taught me to expect in the rutting room, but my fear seems so much easier to handle than the hope sneaking into my heart.

An embarrassing squeak bursts from my throat as the ground disappears out from under *The Submarine*.

He lands on the lower level, ignoring the ladder built into the wall, and continues without missing a stride.

I don't want to give him access to my heart, but if he were the same as the other alphas, he would have savaged me on the deck of the slave market. I can't ignore the restraint he's shown, even if I hate how easily he could decimate my soul.

Hope hurts. That's why I buried it so long ago.

I tell myself that living is enough, but to have an alpha claim and care for me would fulfill my omega heart's deepest desire.

He mentioned offspring. I want younglings with every fiber of my being, but sourness coats my tongue.

The Sisters wanted to breed me, but any babe I birthed would belong to them. They never planned to allow me to raise my younglings.

I blink back tears as *The Submarine* stops and removes his hand from my head. My mind races as he spins the handwheel at the center of a large airtight hatch.

I don't want to be his broodmare if he plans to take my younglings away from me, but I can't imagine this giant, virile male suffering the fragile existence of a babe in his den.

It's safer to send my younglings out of reach, where he can't hurt them. Just the thought of separating from my theoretical children makes my heart ache, but I'll accept his violence alone if it means protecting my offspring.

I jolt out of my musings as he ducks through the hatch into a tiny compartment. He shuts the first door and cranks the wheel until it seals with a hiss. I loosen my grip on his shirt, but duck closer to his chest to avoid scraping along the wall as he pivots to face the other door.

After breaking the watertight seal, he swings the inner hatch open and steps inside.

My core clenches at the delicious pheromones permeating throughout the space. I fill my lungs and hold my breath to savor the scent, but the stench of death wafting from my body ruins the rich bouquet.

He flicks a switch and bathes the room in painfully bright fluorescent light. I flinch and hold my eyes closed as he spins and seals the hatch.

My fear neither heightens nor diminishes as he locks us away from the world. The danger hasn't changed. The sealed door is nothing compared to the submerged vessel. By hauling me onto his ship, he's already ensured I have no escape.

I study the space through my lashes as *The Submarine* sits on one of the two benches lining the walls. Gear hangs from hooks in the ceiling and boxes sit under the benches. The rigid organization unsettles my omega instincts while my logical side appreciates the practicality.

A built-in ladder on the wall opposite the door leads to both an upper and lower level, each with their own watertight hatch, but with levers instead of wheels.

Cold air replaces the arms wrapped around me, but before I can react, the alpha pushes me onto my knees between his legs and uses my hair as a leash to lift my face toward his.

"Take out my cock."

His guttural voice arrows into my abdomen and broadcasts his barely leashed desire while his stiff shoulders and tensed thighs confirm his waning control.

Mouthwatering musk punches into my nostrils. More enticing than the dessert I once earned from The Head Sister, the wet spot on his thigh wafts spicy cinnamon and alpha power.

Yearning fills me. Instinct demands a taste. I lean down and run the flat of my tongue over the soaked fabric.

His groan pulls me deeper into need.

I hiss as he tightens his grip on my hair.

"Don't test me, angel. Take out my cock and put it in your mouth before I rut you on the floor," he rumbles.

My core clenches. Pinching pain plagues my insides. Wetness seeps onto my folds. Saliva floods my mouth.

My hands move without permission. I open his belt with shaky fingers and pop the first button free. The straps of his thigh holsters scratch my shoulders, adding another layer of sensation to my already overstimulated nervous system. The cold floor under my shins barely registers through the heat emanating from his body. His thicker scent dominates my olfactory system, making the stench of blood and death less cloying.

I pull down his zipper. Anticipation and dread war within me.

He lifts his hips. I hook my digits into his waistband and lower his trousers until the holsters prevent me from continuing.

His cock slips free of his pants and bobs in front of my face. I stare in an overwhelmed stupor at his partially engorged knot and thick, veiny shaft.

There's no way that monstrosity will fit inside my body. I'll die. Even the first few inches would split me in two. I'll never survive the entire length *and* the knot at his base.

Disbelief spears through me and a ridiculous half laugh, half scoff, escapes my chest. The Sisters must have never seen an alpha's cock if they thought I could survive being rutted and knotted by a weapon like this.

"Mouth, angel. Now," he snarls and guides my head toward his tip.

As I frantically search for an escape, I notice his fist clenched on the bench beside him. The floor drops out from under me as I glimpse his scarred knuckles.

My omega self wants his protection. His strength. His control.

If taking his cock into my mouth will earn me even a fraction of his power, I'd be an idiot to resist.

And if I lose myself to bliss the moment his taste hits my tongue, I blame it on my encroaching estrous.

Because I can't allow this alpha into my heart. He may dominate my body and dictate my future, but I must protect my sanity. If I'm to survive through the years to come, I'll need every ounce of mental fortitude.

He's too potent. Too addictive. Too delicious.

CHAPTER 4

Port

Her quiet groan of delight vibrates up my shaft and tests my control. I grit my teeth at the sight of her lips stretched around my tip and curl my toes in my boots to hold off a little longer. I need to feel her tight, hot throat around my shaft before I flood her stomach and drench her face with my release.

Knowing I'll push her too far too fast if I lift my hand from the bench, I shift my grip on her hair and lower my growl into a purr of encouragement.

Her eyes dart up to mine before she covers them with her lashes. I add a note of warning to my rumble and tilt my hips, forcing her to take more of my cock. She darts startled eyes up at me.

I study the thin ring of grey barely discernible around her dilated pupils.

Filling my lungs with our mingled pheromones and using the acrid stench of death to maintain my control, I smirk and run my fingers over her scalp, rewarding her for giving me what I want.

My purr melts the stiffness from her body. I enjoy petting her. After a few slow blinks, her brow scrunches and a sliver of awareness seeps into her gaze.

"No teeth. Not this time," I say.

She swallows and flexes her lips around me as though she forgot her predicament. I stroke her hair with a bit too much pressure, pushing her head down and funneling my cock deeper into her mouth. Her jaw tightens. I growl.

"Bite my cock and I'll mark your pussy. Is that what you want, angel? My mating bite between your legs?"

Alarm widens her eyes. She shakes her head. I groan and pull her closer. She tries to push me out with her tongue, but my patience snaps and I surge deeper until she's forced to flatten her tongue. Despite her best efforts, her teeth scrape my shaft as I reach the back of her throat.

She gags. I drop my head back and look at the ceiling, needing a moment to center myself, but hold her down with my tip buried deep in her mouth.

Her nails dig into my thighs.

It's too much.

I wrap both hands around her head and thrust into her throat.

She fights. I fuck in and out anyway, too far gone to deny myself for another moment.

Tears pour down her face and join the mess of spit and precum coating my shaft. Blood drips down my thighs as she sinks her nails into my flesh. Her throat squeezes my cock. An addiction forms.

I snarl and quicken my pace, punching my hips upward as I push her head down and pulling back as I yank her up just far enough for her teeth to graze the sensitive ring behind my tip before plunging right back into her depths.

Beyond words, I mash her lips against my knot and explode. Liquid fire sears the inside of my shaft and spurts from my tip. I shoot my seed down her throat and into her stomach until her hands fall away from my thighs.

Realizing she passed out from lack of oxygen, I lift her just enough to unblock her airway and flood her mouth with my second release. When pearly white fluid seeps from between her lips and runs down my shaft, I snarl and give her head a gentle shake.

She wakes with a jolt and chokes in her confusion, but I dig my nails into her scalp and rub my cock along her tongue until she swallows on reflex. She inhales only to exhale on a wet cough. Seed leaks from her nose.

A thorough mess, she's the most gorgeous thing I've ever seen. I groan and begin shallow, jerky thrusts as another, bigger release builds in my balls.

"Swallow every drop, little angel, or I'll have to start over."

Her nose and brow scrunch in the cutest display of impertinence, but when my cock jerks in her mouth and a fresh wave of seed spurts against the back of her throat, she swallows and emits a blissfully tortured groan.

I hum in approval and enjoy the flexing of her mouth around my pulsing shaft. After I deem she's consumed enough, I yank my cock out and aim my tip at first her cheek, then her nose, then slide her face down my cock and release into her hair, superseding the stench of war and horror wafting from her head.

When the rush of euphoria fades, I drop my head to the wall behind me and close my eyes, enjoying the warmth of her face against the underside of my shaft and the silkiness of her hair covering my crotch.

The lack of her touch on my thighs aggravates me more than the stinging cuts from her nails. I relish the signs of her struggle, even as I bask in the pleasure of holding her head hostage against my cock. Still mostly hard, my shaft continues a slow leak, but my knot partially deflates as the straps of the holsters dig into my legs.

I lift my head and stiffen. With her hands wrapped around both of my knives, her face mashed against my cock, and my hands tangled in her hair, the tiny omega could cause me some serious pain before I took the blades away from her.

Except, she doesn't remove them from the holsters. A stream of fresh warmth trails from her eyes and continues down the underside of my knot. Her shoulders shake.

She caresses the handles before sliding her hands over my thighs and dropping them into her lap.

I pull her away until my cock bobs an inch from her face and study her expression. Despite yearning to see her eyes, I don't demand she open them. I long to preserve her perfection, and the sticky white fluid caked in her lashes may as well be glue.

The thought of her locked in a world of darkness as I ravage and enjoy every inch of her body—inside and out—has me fully hard again.

I extract a hand from her matted hair and ghost a thumb through the mess on her face.

"Why?" I ask.

She shrugs. Too satiated to snarl, I *tsk* and trace her lips.

"You won't get a chance like this again. Why didn't you stab me, angel?"

She wraps her arms around herself and hunches her shoulders.

"You still could, you know. Are you sure you want to pass up this opportunity? You've gotten a taste of how brutal I can be. Don't you want to stop this? Don't you want to be free?"

When she clenches her jaw and takes a shuddering breath through her nose, worry spears through me. I need to see her eyes.

"Open your mouth," I demand. She swallows. Her lashes flutter against her cheek, but despite the tears flowing down her face, my seed prevents her from lifting them.

With dread in every line of her face, she slowly opens her mouth.

I sink three fingers between her teeth and stroke her tongue, ensuring she feels my dominance, before gathering her saliva and swiping the worst of my release from her lashes.

"Open your eyes," I rumble.

An embarrassed flush colors her cheeks as she hiccups. She peels her lids open and reveals her gorgeous grey-ringed pupils.

"Why, little angel? Did I scare you that badly?"

After a shuddering breath, she opens her mouth to speak, but no sound emerges, so she swallows and tries again.

"I'm terrified, but that's not why." Her eyes flit over my face, imploring me to understand, but I need her to explain. "I… I don't…I mean, I can't… I want…" When no other words seem forthcoming, I tilt her head back and slip a knife free of its holster before balancing it on my palm beside her shoulder, giving her easier access. I quirk a brow when she doesn't move.

"You *can*, though, little one. You could have all along. Why didn't you?"

"I don't want to hurt you. I want your protection. Look at the size of your hands. You killed your way through that crowd and you weren't even rampaging. If I—"

I pull her head back even further, flip my hand to grip the blade, and trail the hilt of the knife down her exposed throat.

"Are my hands really what you want to focus on right now, little one?" I ask, tilting my hips and brushing my leaking tip on her chin.

Her nostrils flare as she blinks up at me. Fresh tears seep down her temples.

"I thought I just didn't want to die, but…" she darts her gaze between my eyes, "I think, with you, I…" her lower lip trembles, but she firms her resolve and says, "I might want more."

I toss the knife onto the bench beside me, wrap my hand around her throat, and pull her up to my lips.

So much more delicious with the taste of my musk lingering on her tongue, I consume every inch of her mouth, needing to own her more than I need my next breath. When I finally pull away, her stiff nipples brush against my chest with every heaving breath we share.

Pain tightens her expression. She fists the front of my shirt. Flowery perfume fills the air and slick trickles down her inner thighs.

I groan, pull her legs around my hips, and settle her on my lap. Her pussy lips pillow the underside of my shaft.

Not enough slick.

If I were a lesser alpha, I might fuck her with only the saliva and seed coating my cock, but I refuse to damage my little angel.

She's too important. Too perfect. Too precious.

I need her gushing and desperate before I knot her, but I'm no saint. My control only goes so far.

I dive in for an impossibly deeper kiss and lose myself in her sweetness.

CHAPTER 5

Coral

The hot glide of his cock through my folds detonates mini explosions between my legs. Delicious sensations spread outward from my clit and infect my entire nervous system. A feminine moan fills the air, and jealousy flashes through me until I correlate the vibration in my abused throat with the sound. My jaw, lips, and throat ache from his previous roughness, but the pain is nothing compared to the pulsing in my abdomen.

Drowning in his kiss, I cling to him with all my might, fisting and clawing his shirt until the fabric rips and flesh greets my fingers.

I give back everything he gives me, our tongues dueling and teeth clashing as we each consume the other, but his harsh grip on my breast shocks me into the present.

He squeezes me through the fabric before plucking and twisting my nipple. I whimper and splay my hands over the impressive expanse of his chest, enamored by the sheer size of him and entranced by the play of hard muscles under his scarred flesh. He skims his palm down my side, highlighting my feminine curves with a squeeze of my hip, and sneaks his hand under the hem of my dress.

I gasp as he reaches between our bodies and circles a finger around the sensitive bundle of nerves above my opening. He tilts his hips, rubbing his cock through my folds, and teases either side of my clit, blocking his shaft from stimulating where I want him most. I arch my back and whimper as his hand twists in my hair.

“More?” he murmurs against my lips.

A whine slips from my throat. The sound should embarrass me, but need pounds through my veins. Every cell in my body strives for something I can’t name. Something only he can give me. Something powerful and life changing.

He dips his finger lower. Emptiness plagues my insides. I clench around nothing, making my desperation even worse.

“Are you sure, little angel?”

Blood wells underneath my digits as I claw at his chest.

His chuckle vibrates through me.

Desire squeezes the breath from my lungs as he draws designs along my sex and teases my entrance. I squirm, unable to breathe, and seek his mouth, but he leans away, shifting the hard rod between my legs and bumping my clit.

I ride the waves, but it's not nearly enough. I need more. So much more.

The world narrows to where our bodies touch. Delicious pressure grows between my legs. I hiss as his finger sinks into my body. The stretching hurts so good. I need more, even though fear ices my spine.

He adds a second finger.

I can't breathe. The pinnacle lies just out of reach. A little more and I'd detonate. One stroke over my clit. The curl of his fingers inside me. A lick on the shell of my ear.

I need these things. All of them. Now.

"More?" he asks in a slightly mocking tone, but the gruffness scrambles my senses and I whimper again.

He adds a third finger. I push, pull, writhe, and dig my knees into his hips, overwhelmed by the painful yet glorious stretching. It's too much. It's not enough.

I teeter on the edge of a cliff.

"More?"

His rumble nearly sends me over.

"Say it," he growls.

"Please," I beg.

"Fuck, angel, I can't—"

I grind myself lower onto his fingers until the calluses on his palm mash my clit.

The world spins. Frigid, textured metal digs into my back. Hot, hard alpha covers my front.

I'm empty. So empty.

The broad head of his cock settles between my folds. Wetness leaks from me, but when he pushes forward, a pain pulls a hiss from my lips.

My alpha's teeth and tongue capture my mouth, promising pleasure beyond my imagination. I give myself to him, knowing a fight would be futile. He's so big. So strong.

Too big. Too strong.

A feminine voice cries out as he forces the tip of his dick through my entrance. He invades further and further, stretching and filling me in one slow, ruthless thrust, until his partially engorged knot squashes my pussy lips.

"Too much. Stop. Please," I whisper, too far gone to climb higher yet unable to jump into bliss.

"You asked for this, baby. No going back now. You're mine. My female. My omega. My fallen angel."

He pushes me over the edge with several brutal yet controlled thrusts of his hips. Fireworks burst behind my closed eyelids and electricity shoots from my core to my extremities. The glide of his massive cock as he invades and retreats shatters my higher thoughts and drowns me in sensation.

When my diaphragm finally relaxes enough for me to pull in a breath, I blink open crusty eyes and meet terrifying black orbs. Without a trace of his irises visible, his eyes offer me a view into the darkest of underworlds.

"How much farther will you fall with me, angel? This isn't enough. Not nearly enough. I need more."

My vision blanks white and agony spears between my legs when he shoves himself deeper. His next thrust hurts impossibly worse. Fresh tears pour down my temples and I push against his chest as his partially inflated knot stretches my entrance. White-hot fissures of misery warn of tissues tearing if he doesn't stop.

I whimper and silently beg for salvation.

The devil delivers in his own way.

I launch into a brand-new world of dark depravity. He pins my knees to my shoulders and sets a merciless rhythm, pulling so far out his flange stretches my entrance before funneling back in so hard his tip hits a painfully sensitive spot deep within me. I writhe and fight for breath as he pummels my body against the floor. The violence nourishes my omega beast despite the terror jangling within me.

Expecting his gigantic knot to rip me to pieces, I'm too scared to orgasm, yet too full to ignore the pleasure and pain roaring through me.

He stops with only half his shaft pulsing within my pussy. I stare in shock as scorching hot liquid spurts from his tip and floods my insides despite his engorged knot being outside my body. The angry red bulge pains my omega heart.

He snarls and wraps his fist around the base of his cock before he yanks his cock out of my pussy. I extract my nails from his arms and watch stupidly as he covers my mons and the back of my thighs with his release.

With jerky movements, he breaks the straps of my shift and yanks the fabric down to bare my breasts. Heat pulses low in my abused abdomen as pearly white fluid splashes onto my nipples and trails down my pale curves.

He scrunches my dress in his hand and marks my stomach with his seed. The sight of my belly button filled with his release sends a surge of delight through my omega heart. My insides throb and fluid gushes from my opening, but very little slick joins his cum.

Fatigue and frustration sap the energy from my limbs, so I relax against the floor, uncaring about the uncomfortable position.

The Submarine's features slingshot into my subconscious. I'll never be free of him. He owns me now, even without marking or knotting me.

I never once entertained the idea of an alpha with such restraint. To fuck an omega on the verge of heat, but not knot her, goes against all expectations.

His control breaks my defenses quicker than anything else ever could.

Yes, it hurt. A lot.

But I'm not broken and bleeding, just sore and overwhelmed.

"What do I call you?" I ask.

"Alpha. Master. Satan. King of assholes," he mumbles as he settles his hips between my splayed legs and lowers himself to his elbows, framing my head with his forearms.

His sardonic tone doesn't register before my mouth moves without permission.

"No, I mean, what's your name?"

"Why do you want to know, so you can curse me when I lose control and ravage you again?"

I blink up at him, my thoughts too far away for me to register the emotions in his voice.

"No, I need a name for my savior."

He quirks a brow and brushes my hair back with achingly gentle strokes. Such gigantic, powerful hands shouldn't be capable of such tenderness.

My breath hitches and a stray tear seeps down my temple.

"I don't think savior is the right word to describe me, angel."

"It is, though. None of the alphas at the slave market would have done what you just did. They would have knotted any and all of my holes the second they had the chance." Fury darkens his eyes as he grinds his jaw, but I can't stop my wayward mouth. "Whoever bought my first heat wouldn't have shown such restraint, even with The Sisters overseeing the process. You—"

His hand covers the bottom half of my face, cutting me off and smearing the goop caked on my chin, and he leans down to growl in my ear.

"I shouldn't have fucked you at all. Your body isn't ready yet, but I couldn't stop myself, so don't make me into a saint." He loosens his grip on my face and wipes the tear off my temple with his other thumb. "I can't handle those innocent eyes staring so sweetly up at me. They make me want to do unspeakable things to you, little angel."

What little saliva left in my mouth dries up. No more tears spill from my lashes, despite the lump in my throat.

His refusal to see my point of view only solidifies his goodness in my eyes.

He may have stolen, terrified, and hurt me, but he hasn't injured me. He hasn't crushed my spirit. He hasn't used and discarded me.

I swallow.

My periphery fades to black. A cramp steals through my midsection, but no slick gushes from my pussy. I reach up and grab his sides, but my strength wanes and I lose my grasp on his shirt.

The moment he senses something wrong, he pulls me into his lap. With his pants tangled in his holsters and the benches so close together, the position proves more than awkward for him, but he angles his shoulders and wedges his knees against the opposite bench and wraps me in his arms.

For the first time in my life, I bask in a warm, living cocoon. It's the best nest in the universe and I never want to leave.

A low, angry rumble leaves my chest as my perch moves. I fight the encroaching darkness, but a circle consumes my periphery and shrinks toward the center of my vision. I close my eyes, but my alpha shakes my shoulders.

A sweet and citrusy smell tingles my nostrils.

"Drink," he demands.

The cold rim of a container presses against my bottom lip. I open my mouth despite just wanting to sleep.

Cool liquid shocks my tastebuds into overdrive, and I suck down the beverage as fast as he allows.

As my body absorbs the sugar, I sigh as yet another realization hits me.

The Submarine recognized my dehydration before I did. After hours of straining in my cage, surrounded by alpha stink and sweating in the blistering sun, my body used up all the water I drank this morning. My oncoming estrous only compounded my dilemma.

He knew. That's why he didn't knot me.

It's also why he offers me a second drink, this one plain water, but the crisp flavor baffles me.

I've never had such clean water before. Even without my sight, I know it lacks the reddish tinge of what The Sisters hauled into my room each day.

I lift my lids to check the container but drown in intense amber eyes. Whoever gave him such thick lashes has earned all my praise and worship.

"Name?" I manage despite the heaviness of my tongue.

"Port. My name is Port. And yours?"

"Coral."

His deep rumble turns my bones to slush, and I close my eyes to savor the sensation. My heart thuds against my sternum. Need pulses deep in my abdomen, but I wince from the swollen tissues between my legs.

Thick fingers grasp my chin. I open my eyes.

"Be careful how you wield it, little angel," my alpha says.

For a moment, I stare blankly up at him.

Wield what? I don't have a weapon, and even if I did, haven't I already proven I won't hurt him? One knife remains in his holster while the other teeters on the edge of the bench beside his shoulder.

His eyes dip to my lips and understanding dawns.

He chuckles and rubs his thumb along my lower lip.

Emotions too big to understand swell within my chest.

He gave me something no one else ever thought of giving me. I never imagined I'd receive such a precious gift, no matter how warped it may be.

By telling me his name, he gave me power over him. He willingly offered me a way to leave my mark on his soul.

He stole me. Terrorized me. Hurt me.

He also slaughtered his way through a crowd, showed me a gentleness I thought couldn't exist in this world, and proved himself more humane than any other alpha on the surface.

The Submarine is mine. My alpha. My Port.

As he shifts around to remove his holsters, boots, and pants, I bury my face in his shirt and breathe through the storm whirling through my soul. My heat returns, and because of the hydration my alpha offered me, fresh slick accompanies each painful cramp. His hard cock grinds against my ass and encourages more wetness from my depths, but he ignores the calling of my body and yanks his shirt over his head.

I slip further into madness as his bare chest spans the width of my gaze. I need him. Every inch of him.

He's mine.

The only doubt left within me is the niggling worry of being nothing but a broodmare. If I attach my soul to his and he steals my younglings from me, my omega heart will shatter into a million irreparable pieces.

No matter how much control he gives me, I'm powerless against the strength of his body.

I must endear him to me somehow, so when the time comes, he won't become the heartless devil he claims to be.

I'll make him want to give me what my omega soul yearns for.

A doting alpha. Arms overflowing with precious babes. Love.

A family. Happiness.

More. Always more.

With him.

Somehow.

CHAPTER 6

Port

Her shaking worsens with each passing second. The jiggling of her breasts proves too tantalizing, so I spread the fabric of her dress over her to hide the most tempting bits and grab the emergency stash of fluids from the box under the bench. I sling the bag over my shoulder before standing and kicking my discarded clothes and the empty bottles into a pile and heading toward the ladder.

The bottles clink together as I move her from a cradle hold to press her front against mine. I wrap her legs around my waist and her arms around my neck.

"Hold on, little angel. It's a tight fit."

My cock jerks at my innuendo, but I ignore both it and her wet, silky pussy brushing against my abdomen and climb the first few rungs of the ladder before reaching above us and twisting the lever.

I swing the hatch upward and secure it to the wall so it stays open. With a few calculated rolls of my shoulders, I work my way through the hole and continue up the ladder until I reach the upper level. When I step onto the floor and pivot away from the ladder, my omega makes a surprised sound in the back of her throat. My shaft pounds in response, but I stride across the space and set her on the counter.

"Don't move," I warn before stomping back and locking the hatch.

A panel of glass on the left reveals the wet room. With the tiled floor already filled with water, the narrow bench glimmers under the surface. Dozens of showerheads line the ceiling, and although none are on, the sound of running water echoes through the chamber.

My omega leans over and twists the sink faucet handle. Her stunned expression as she watches crystal clear water splash into the basin fills me with pride.

"How?" she asks, more to herself than to me.

I push her knees apart and press my thighs to the edge of the counter, letting my cock bob against her stomach, but don't pull her close for fear of losing control again. As she continues to stare at the water, I place the sack on the counter and fish out another bottle of juice.

She jerks when I press the glass to her lips, but dutifully swallows when I cup the back of her head and tip the drink into her mouth.

Her pallor lifts and her cheeks flush pink.

The need to see her in all her naked, ethereal beauty, without blood, guts, and jizz obscuring the paleness of her flesh, pulls a snarl from me. I yank her close and snatch the bag off the counter before sliding open the glass door and stepping down into the bath. After setting the drinks on the ledge, I shut the glass and pin her against the wall beside the shower controls.

I shield her with my body as I adjust the water temperature. When steam fogs the glass and the surface of the bath warms to match the showers, I turn and lower us both onto the bench.

Filth swirls around our hips before the current pulls it toward the grate underneath the shower control panel. I stroke her hair away from her brow and enjoy the slow progression of my seed as it slips down her face, neck, and shoulders. The torn straps of her dress hang over her breasts and the fabric clings to her curves, defying gravity.

Her pink nipples show through the thin material.

I distract my hands by reaching for the liquid soap. Her bottom lip disappears between her teeth as she sneaks one last taste of my seed from her lips before it slips away, but when I squirt a dollop of fragrant soap onto my palm, her nostrils flare and she releases her lip.

Her dainty fingers cling to my shoulders as I shift her out of the direct spray of water and scrub the shampoo over her scalp. I tilt my hips, grinding the underside of my shaft against her soft stomach, and purr in delight as she gives herself to my care. Every hair follicle receives the utmost attention as I draw designs over her head, enjoying the growing suds and slippery glide of my fingers through her locks.

When white froth runs down her brow, I lean forward and support her head in one hand while slicking the water away from her face as the shower rinses her hair.

Pure white from the roots, her hair nearly blinds me in the bright lights.

She must truly be an angel.

I dragged her into hell, fucked her throat, and rutted her on the floor, but I'm nowhere near done overseeing her ruination. She's got so much further to fall.

With her hair rinsed, I pull her front flush against mine and rub her nipples against my chest through the fabric. Her wanton moan shoves me toward mania, but I need her completely bare and washed of all traces of others.

She'll be mine and only mine.

"Close your eyes," I growl through gritted teeth.

With the tip of my cock protruding from the water, the scent of my seed overrides the floral soap, giving away my desperation.

She closes her eyes. Her obedience tests me in ways I never thought possible. I swallow and grab the soap off the ledge.

After rolling the bar in my hand enough to lather my digits, I set it on the ledge and run my fingers over her face. Careful to avoid her eyes, I wash her features in a half daze, unwilling to break free of her spell, until thick trails of soap run down her throat. I lean her into the spray and rinse her face, paying special attention to her lashes, until not a trace of grime remains above her neck.

Lust pulses down my spine.

Her shift slips off her right breast.

I groan and palm her left breast, torturing us both by holding the fabric in place and kneading her with my fingers. She arches her back, rubbing her nipple against my hand and grinding her pussy against the underside of my shaft.

"Please, alpha," she whispers, barely loud enough for me to hear her over the rushing water.

I snarl and push her off my lap before bending down and yanking her head closer until her ear lines up with my lips.

"The next time I sink my cock into you, my knot will follow. You'll be locked on my dick for days and leak my seed for weeks. Don't test me, angel, or we'll both drown in this bath."

On her knees with her nipples teasing the surface of the water, she's the most splendid creature I've ever seen, but when she aims wide, lustful eyes up at me, I look away.

She tempts me too much. My alpha beast lurks a hairsbreadth beyond my control, ready to burst free and fuck her into the afterlife.

I uncap a bottle of water, grab her arm, and tug her onto the bench beside me, careful to put an inch between our hips so I don't snap. When she clutches her hands in her lap, I fist her hair and ensure she drinks the entire bottle before releasing her.

I snatch the bar of soap off the ledge, pry her fingers apart, cup her hand in mine, and drop the soap onto her upturned palm.

"Finish washing yourself while I watch," I demand.

She stares at the soap for a prolonged moment, and I wonder if she's testing me, but when she lifts her gaze, I find no trace of guile.

"I've never..." she stalls and darts her eyes around the shower, obviously at a loss for words.

"You've never teased an alpha before? Good. I want to take all your firsts."

"No, I've never showered before. Or had soap. It was always just a bucket of rusty water and a sponge."

Time stands still as she shows me her uncertainty. The vulnerability shining from her eyes clamps a fist around my heart and squeezes until I can't breathe.

The gift she gives me awakens bittersweet emotions within my alpha soul. I long to pamper and spoil her. To rut and knot her. To breed and build a loving, supportive family with her.

To tie our hearts and secure our futures together.

I growl and pull her to me by her throat. Water splashes up my torso as I stop centimeters before her breasts collide with my front.

"This is all yours now, Coral. We can visit anytime. You can shower whenever you please, with only one rule," I promise.

Her breath hitches and she swallows. The delicate column of her throat shifts in my grasp.

"What's the rule?" she asks in a breathy voice.

I skim my nose down her temple and whisper in her ear.

"I get to watch, touch, and take whenever I please."

Her eyes glaze and she bobbles her head in mindless agreement as a cramp tightens her midsection.

"Fuck, baby, you're being such a good girl. I want to knot you right here," I moan before licking the shell of her ear and sitting back. "But you owe me a show. Lather up, little angel, so I can cover you in my seed again."

Sorrow flashes across her features, but fear chases it away as she glances down at my jutting cock. With my knot mostly inflated, my veins pulse along my shaft and my tip darkens to an angry red.

She stumbles back and slips, but I catch her elbow and guide her to stand between two showerheads, so the least amount of water rains down on her.

When I sit back and brace my arms along the ledge behind me, desire smolders in the thin ring of grey around her pupils.

She shifts her gaze to the bar of soap in her hand and studies it for a moment before trying to roll it between her fingers, but her digits are too short and it slips free. With an embarrassed flush, she drops to her knees and captures the bar before it sinks to the tiles.

Her innocence pierces my heart and drains the pus festering within. I'll never spend a night alone again.

I have this sweet little angel to keep me company.

Forever.

CHAPTER 7

Coral

His voice echoes in my head. One word. My name.

The combination proves disastrous. I can't string two words together because of it.

Which makes my new endeavor baffling.

I rise onto unsteady legs and gnaw on my bottom lip. I should strike a pose or do *something* to make the moment more sensual, but I don't know what. The Sisters always said my scent alone would capture any alpha's attention, but this isn't just any alpha. This is *The Submarine*. My forever mate. My Port.

I need to make him want me so badly he'll do anything to protect my physical health *and* my mental wellbeing. If he breeds me, I need to nurture my babies myself, not pass them off to a wet nurse.

The soap squishes between my fingers as I stand like a dullard in the center of the shower.

Nothing comes to mind, so I touch my shoulder.

The slippery glide shocks me. I forget to think and explore my body as I've never wanted to before, running my hands down my arms, up my sides, along my ribs, and down my soft stomach to the curve of my hips. It's not enough. I skim my fingertips up my belly and cup my breasts. My entire world changes as I pinch my nipples and soft, sensual sensations roll through me.

All the while, lust-darkened amber eyes watch with burning intensity and a masculine rumble encourages me to continue my exploration.

I trail my hands down to the juncture of my thighs and gasp as electricity zaps through my clit. Too sensitive for more, I continue to sink lower and play in the slick gathered between my swollen folds.

The low vibration morphs. I move my hands away from my pussy and clean my legs instead, but even without direct stimulation, my sex pulses in need.

When soap covers every inch of me, I step under the nearest showerhead and let the downpour rinse it away.

I can't stop staring at my alpha's long, muscular arms stretched across the back of the bench. His presence alone dominates the space, and my heart simultaneously quails and celebrates. His broad chest tapers down to ridged abdominals and a slightly narrower waist, while his thick thighs and imposing cock perfect his alpha physique.

My mouth waters as my heart quivers.

"Good girl. Now wash me," he growls.

I hesitate. His knuckles turn white on the tiles. A wave of heat rolls up from my toes to my ears, clenching my womb along the way. The perfume of my slick overpowers the scent of soap.

I blink as tears fill my eyes. The shower is too big. Too exposed. Too cold. I need a nest.

Remembering the comfort of his arms cocooning me away from the world, I stumble toward him.

He catches me by the shoulders and prevents me from burrowing against his chest.

"Not yet, little angel. Wash me. Touch me. Worship me. I am your god down here," he growls.

A sob wrenches from my chest, but my hands itch to obey his command. I rub the soap in both hands before dropping it on the ledge behind his shoulder and splaying my fingers over his chest.

With my tears and slick almost as prevalent as the water raining down on us, I test the resilience of his flesh and marvel at the rock-hard muscles underneath. His scars hurt my heart, and without thinking, I lean down and press my lips against the one on his shoulder, needing to soothe the pain even though the wound healed long ago. The sting of soap on my lips only encourages me to find the next scar. And the next.

Down his arm. Over his wrist. Each knuckle. The inside of his forearm. His ribs.

He stops me from going lower. His chest expands and contracts with rapid breaths.

I kiss the round scar above his heart. Sadness squeezes my throat as I imagine this massive, powerful alpha as a younger version of himself with a raw, gaping wound after being stabbed with what must have been rebar.

Thin white scars cover so much of him. I continue upward, stopping where his shoulder meets his neck to enjoy the pheromones wafting from him, before leaving a trail of soft pecks up the side of his throat.

His purr deepens. My slick thickens and pain radiates from my womb, but I can't stop. I must kiss the pain away from the scar on his face.

The stubble on his chin scratches my lips. A shiver runs down my spine. My nipples brush against his chest.

I sweep my lips side to side over the lowest part of his scar. He stops moving. Stops breathing.

With pain and awe overflowing my heart, I kiss every millimeter of his once torn flesh until I reach the top of his scar.

Needing to rid myself of the taste of soap, I lick his cheek.

It isn't enough.

My body moves on instinct, climbing into his lap and clutching his shoulders as I sneak another lick. I lower my aim, enjoying the different textures of his face.

The silkiness of his lips intrigues me the most. I flick my tongue over the raised scar. Test his bottom lip. Trace the seam of his mouth.

His control breaks.

I gasp as he fists my hair and demands full use of my mouth. His tongue invades and retreats, urging mine to dance along. He grabs my ass and grinds the underside of his shaft through my folds. Water swirls and splashes around our hips.

He stands. I wrap my legs around his waist, trapping his cock between our bodies. My breasts flatten against his chest. Water sluices over us as he stalks through the downpour.

He releases my hair, turns off the shower, and goes right back to dominating my mouth with his.

Too caught up in the haze of lust to notice the world beyond my alpha, I ignore our surroundings and writhe against him, demanding more. More kisses. More friction. More pleasure. More pain.

He nips my bottom lip.

"Be still, little angel, or I'll knot you against the wall."

I whine. I want.

He hisses and pulls my hair, aiming my face up to the ceiling, exposing my neck, and forcing me to listen.

"I'm climbing down the ladder. Don't move," he snarls.

I writhe, needing his hard shaft inside me, not pressed against my stomach.

"Stop grinding that hot, wet pussy against me before I deny you my knot again. Is that what you want, baby? My seed spilling from your cunt instead of filling up your womb?"

A whine, impossibly more pathetic than before, fills the air. I shake my head and groan as the movement pulls the hair in his grasp.

"Then be still. Can you do that for me, Coral? Can you stop moving, just for a little while?"

I whimper, tuck my face where his throat meets his shoulder, grab my elbows behind his neck, and dig my heels into his sides, lifting myself higher on his chest so his cock springs free and bops against my ass instead of stimulating my clit.

"Good girl."

His praise clenches my core. Slick gushes down his front. He curses and descends the ladder with quick movements.

I dig my nails into my forearms as the friction between our bodies scrambles my mind. The hardness of his chest against my sensitive nipples sends fissures of electricity straight to my womb.

He stops moving. I press my nose against his jugular and breathe in his fiery pheromones. He reaches for his nape and peels my arms apart. I hiss as he wraps his fingers around my throat and forces me away from his delicious scent.

Another pathetic whimper leaves my chest as he kneels and pushes my legs to the ground.

"Nest, little angel," he snarls.

I stare at his massive shoulders and muscular arms, wanting only them, but he weaves his digits into my hair, pinches my chin, and guides my attention to the side.

Disbelief spears through me. There's no way this is real. I must be hallucinating.

The same footprint as the entire bath level—including the shower, sinks, and closet—this room has the most space I've seen since entering his ship, but stacks and stacks of nesting materials line the walls and crowd the square footage until only a path wide enough for my alpha to sidestep to the center remains.

My omega heart squeals in joy and sobs in wonder while my body merely stares in shock.

“Nest, Coral.”

Animalistic fury sparks through me and I lash out, pushing his hands and stepping away before crowding him like a lunatic.

“That’s the third time you’ve said my name. You’re not allowed to say it anymore.” I poke his chest and snarl. “I don’t like it.” I lie, but I poke his chest harder and continue. “I can’t stand it.” Another lie. Another poke. “It’s not fair!”

Sudden sobs break from my chest. I fling my arms around his neck.

Still kneeling, he doesn’t budge despite my insanity. He wraps his brawny arms around me and crushes me against him for a moment before peeling me off him and setting me at arm’s length.

“Another first?” he asks.

I nod, but I’m not sure if he means my heat-induced insanity or if he can sense the real reason behind my turmoil. I’ve never made a proper nest. The most materials The Sisters allowed me were a pillow, sheet, and blanket. A flash of heat steals my breath.

Port rises to his feet, turns me by my shoulders, gathers my hair in his hand, and uses it as a leash to guide me to the center of the room.

A bare mattress sits all alone. One pillow and one sheet lie folded near the head. Loneliness wafts from the area.

I grunt in surprise when my alpha shoves me face first onto the bed. He wraps his forearm under my hips and lifts me to my knees while keeping the side of my face mashed against the mattress.

His knot bops my ass. He releases my hips and scratches his nails up the back of my thigh as he whispers in my ear.

"You've got so much further to fall, angel. Build a nest so you have somewhere soft to land after I fuck you senseless and fill you with my seed."

He disappears. The air is too cold.

Fabric plops onto my head.

While faint traces of my alpha's scent waft from the fabric, it isn't enough to satisfy my omega needs. I snarl, sit up, and toss the blanket at the idiot in question.

"More," I snarl.

He quirks a brow. I pull the used pillow and sheet into a hug, bury my face inside, and hum in delight.

"Ah. More. Ask nicely, little omega."

I don't want to.

I peek out of the bundle but keep my nose and mouth covered. My muffled growl holds so much feminine fury my hackles rise, triggering a deeper layer of instincts hidden within me.

With the promise of retaliation in every move, *The Submarine* rubs the blanket over his chest and shoulders, never taking his eyes from mine.

Chills and heat alternate down my spine. My abused insides throb in remembered pain, but I can't back down from the challenge. I need the tension between myself and this giant alpha.

Every moment he caters to my will is another moment I dig my claws deeper into his heart. Maybe, with enough intensity, I can break through his defenses and become indispensable, not only in body, but also in spirit.

He's already stolen my heart.

I need him. I want him.

He's mine.

My alpha. My Submarine. My Port.

Mine.

Forever.

CHAPTER 8

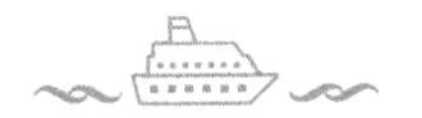

Port

I toss the blanket at her and snatch another off the nearest pile.

She breaks eye contact to bury her face in the new fabric, but after a few sniffs, she lifts her head again.

"More," she snarls.

My cock pulses, and wetness seeps from my tip. I fist my shaft through the blanket and groan as her eyes flare. Need reddens her cheeks. She kneads the mound in her arms.

"Not until you start nesting, little angel," I say, shifting the fabric to mark a different section and to prevent myself from giving it to her.

She glares at me for half a second before another cramp distracts her. Before the pain ebbs, her body moves, her estrous in full force and leading her movements.

With lithe grace, she spreads the freshly scented blanket over the mattress before layering the sheet over the top. Kneeling in the center, she sticks the pillow between her legs and grinds her leaking pussy against it.

Envious beyond belief, I throw the newly marked blanket at her and snatch a pillow off the stack behind me.

As I smear precum over both sides, she fluffs the slick-covered pillow into place near the head of the bed and scrunches the third blanket near the foot.

Her constant low rumble pleases me to no end. She sinks deeper into instincts, letting out little sounds of delight as I drop item after item onto her head. After clearing two stacks—one of folded linen and the other pillows—curiosity gets the better of me and I grab the basket of odds and ends near the ladder.

I rub my scent over a doll with no face, three stuffed animals—each missing at least one limb, if not all four—a rug, and an oddly shaped cushion.

When she runs out of new things to stack, she growls and looks up from her creation.

Confusion wrinkles her brow until mirth lights her face. She bites her bottom lip before crawling to the edge of the mattress.

"More?" she asks.

Her eyes flit from my face to the objects in my arms.

"Say please," I growl.

She licks her lips. My cock jerks.

"Please?"

Without an ounce of artifice in her entire body, she steals chunks of my soul with her white hair, pale flesh, blown pupils, pert breasts, and wide hips.

"Try again, angel," I challenge.

"More, please, alpha," she says. Her fingers absently knead the nearest fabric. Slick drenches the half-formed nest underneath her.

"Almost, but not quite what I want," I rumble.

My foot inches closer without my permission, but I dare not call it back.

"Please, Port? More?"

I groan and catch the fresh spurt of seed on the cushion before tossing the toys into the center of the nest. She rushes to claim her prizes. Her gorgeous ass tempts me to drop to my knees and take her from behind, but I finish marking the rug and add it to her collection.

Needing a moment to center myself, but unwilling to put much distance between us, I stalk to the metal box attached to the wall beside the ladder, open the lid, and yank several random food pouches from the selection before stomping back to her.

The toys and cushion add lumps to the edges of the nest, but she stares down in disgust at the rug draped over the corner.

I reach down to take it, but she snatches it away with a hiss and tucks it under the mound near the makeshift footboard, ensuring we'll never touch it, but including it in her creation.

Longing fills her gaze when she glances at the nearby stacks.

I can't deny her, not with her sweet voice echoing my name in my head. After dropping the food packets beside the bed, I drench countless items in my pheromones. Curtains, quilts, rugs, toys, everything I hoarded throughout the years becomes hers. She builds us the most luxurious nest in the entire universe. I watch in awe as she works.

When she disappears between the layers and ceases her purr, I stiffen.

The silence proves daunting.

This tiny, resilient little angel already owns my heart. I have yet to knot and claim her, but there's no doubt I'm already smitten.

I'll do anything for her.

Anything.

Without prompting, she sticks her fingers out from between the layers of the nest, wiggles them, and begs.

"Please, Port? I need you."

As I climb into her cocoon, careful not to destroy it with my wide shoulders, the full bouquet of her perfume hits me in the face.

I don't know how she waited this long. On her hands and knees, slick pours down her thighs and soaks the material underneath her. She wriggles her hips and fists the pillow in desperation.

I add a note of comfort to my growl and guide her onto her back. She resists until I settle my weight over her. Her groan signals the end of my restraint.

In a flurry of dark sensuality, I explore every inch of her, my hands too rough and my mouth too hungry, but she writhes underneath me, demanding more. I cannot resist. Cannot deny her. Cannot stand to see her suffer.

I wedge my shoulders between her legs and feast on her slick, licking her clit and stroking her insides with my fingers. She flies apart under my tongue. I consume her release.

It isn't enough. Her estrous rallies and demands fulfillment.

I crawl up her body, fit my tip to her entrance, and frame her head with my hands. She writhes, testing my predatory drive, until I snarl, sink half an inch into her pussy, and nip her bottom lip. The moment she offers me her blown pupils, I surge into her with one brutal thrust until my partially inflated knot catches on her pussy lips.

Her open mouth calls to me. Neither of us needs to breathe anyway, so I join our mouths and rule her from top to bottom with my tongue and cock, syncing my invasion and retreat. Slick squelches every time I seat myself within her, and after a few strokes, her cream coats my knot and drips down my legs.

I yank my mouth away from hers and nip her earlobe.

"Are you ready for my knot, little angel?"

She shakes her head while tilting her hips, saying no, but giving me easier access to her depths.

"I'm going to fill that sweet little pussy with my cum until you ache with it, and when you think you can't handle anymore, I'll play with your clit and pump more into you as you orgasm around me. My seed will have nowhere to go until my knot pops free, but guess what, little omega?" Her nails sink into my chest. I lick the soft flesh under her ear and nip her lobe harder. "I'll just knot you again and again until my seed takes root and you swell with my offspring." Her whimper undoes me. "Fuck, Coral, I can't wait. Take all of me like a good girl."

She does, arching and scratching, whimpering and hissing, giving me everything as I slowly work my knot deeper and deeper into her body. When her entrance finally relaxes enough, I snarl and snap my hips forward, fully seating myself. With my knot fully expanded behind her pubic bone, the spongy ring of her cervix clamps around my tip.

She screams and shatters. Her entire body seizes.

I sink my teeth into her shoulder and die a million glorious deaths. Wave after wave of bliss erupts from my balls and scorches the inside of my shaft before jettisoning from my tip. Euphoria clouds my mind as the metallic taste of her blood coats my tongue. Our bond snaps into place, not complete, but brilliant in its uniqueness.

For what feels like millennia but must only be minutes, I spill my seed straight into her womb and pour my joy into her soul.

When her orgasm ends, I lick the wound on her shoulder and cup the back of her head to guide her mouth to my chest, but she lunges upward and sinks her teeth into my flesh without prompting, covering the circular scar over my heart.

Pain and pleasure collide. Our bond glows in completion. I purr and roll onto my back, destroying our nest, but I tug the layers over us and wrap my arms around her.

She falls asleep between one breath and the next. Pride flows through me.

With unhindered access to both her body and soul, I stroke her back and bask in her feminine presence.

Even blissed out while locked on my knot and exhausted from my rutting, fear and dread linger within her.

I must erase them.

Her stomach rumbles.

I'll feed her. She won't want it, since she's in full estrous, but she needs the calories, so I'll ensure she eats.

I stop petting her and close my eyes, both to enjoy the moment of peace and to encourage my knot to deflate. With an audible pop, it slips free. She jolts awake.

I roll us over, pin her knees to her ears, bury my face between her legs, and consume the first gush of our combined essences. She wriggles and whines. I give in and ferry a mouthful to her lips. She accepts my offering with pure omega joy, humming and licking my tongue with eager little flicks.

I duck down for another taste, but stop a few inches away and enjoy the view.

"Gods, little angel, your pussy is so pretty leaking my cum." I run my thumb through the mess and push my seed back into her. "I can't wait to fill you up again." Her pussy tightens around my digit. I pull out and lower my face. She bucks and grabs my head.

I share, carrying mouthfuls to her lips until only a trickle seeps from her pussy.

Her stomach rumbles again.

I pull her onto my chest, wrap the remnants of our nest around us, and snag a food packet from the floor. She turns her head away, but I snarl and use her hair to keep her facing in the right direction.

"Just a few bites, little angel, then I'll knot you again."

She sighs, nods, and opens her mouth. I feed her from my hand, enjoying her reaction to each bite of dried fruit, nuts, and cheese.

A bubble of intimacy forms around us. More relaxed than ever before, I bask in her perfection and relish the start of our new future together.

She flushes. Her cramps return.

We spend days locked together. I cherish every moment. She spoils me with her sweetness and surprises me with flashes of feistiness. I enjoy every challenge she presents and bask in the quiet moments. When her heat breaks, I fall into a doze and hold her close.

I wake and shift her off my chest. She gives a halfhearted whine, but I tuck the filthy blankets around her and she settles back to sleep.

I wrap a sheet around my hips and climb the ladder to the outer hatch. In less than five minutes, I lock the inner door and return to my omega.

She sighs when I pull her from the nest and gather her into a cradle carry. Emotions clog my throat as she cuddles against my chest. Her trust floors me.

I shift her weight and climb one-handed up the ladder and don't stop even after I sit on the bench in the bath. She pouts at the coolness of the water, but I clean us both with quick efficiency and dress her in the cleanest dirty sleep set I have. The t-shirt and shorts dwarf her, but she pulls the collar to her nose and scents my faded pheromones.

"More?"

Her groggy voice and hazy eyes make me reconsider my decision, but her angst infects our bond too much for me to change my mind.

I whip my shirt off her head and rub the fabric over my front. She grumbles and pushes it away when I try to fit it over her head.

"More," she demands.

I smirk and stroke my cock through the fabric. She accepts it with a crooked smile.

I enjoy the weight of her eyes on me as I pull on my pants.

As though my approach jolts her awake, she snaps into awareness.

"Why are we getting dressed?"

"We're going out for a moment."

The worry tightening her features solidifies my decision. I step between her knees and pull her against my chest.

"Why?" she asks as I lift her off the counter and head toward the ladder.

"To meet someone."

She stiffens, but drops her forehead to my chest and wraps her legs around me as I climb down the ladder.

I open the inner hatch and wedge my bulk into the watertight chamber. Her fingers tremble against my nape.

"Hush, little angel. This is what's best."

She shakes her head and clings tighter to me. I sigh and release the handwheel on the outer door to fill my hands with her ass.

"What are you thinking, Coral?"

"I'm tired and don't want to go out," she mumbles against my chest.

I squeeze her ass and rumble out a warning. Her nipples pebble and slick scents the air.

She darts her head up and meets my eyes. When her nostrils flare, I understand her surprise.

"Yes, baby, you're pregnant."

She blinks. Swallows. Blinks again.

"Our first mating... my first heat..."

I chuckle and shift one hand to her nape.

"Yes, little omega. I filled you so full of my seed you had no choice. You'll birth our first offspring in a few months."

She blinks several more times before reality settles over her. Tears drip from her snowy lashes and trail down her pale cheeks.

"Then why are we leaving our den? I need—"

I end her question with a kiss and don't pull back until we're both breathless.

"This is important. Trust me?"

As she studies my expression, her apprehension grows, but she nods and tucks the side of her face against my chest. I open the outer hatch before shifting her higher and bracing my forearm under my ass. She gives a hesitant sigh and focuses on my heartbeat as I pin her head to my sternum and duck through the halls until I reach the common room.

Male pheromones linger in the space, but only two beta females sit on the cushioned bench along the far wall. They stand to greet us, but wisely keep as much distance as the room allows.

I nod, settle in the swivel chair at the end of the table, and plant my feet to keep my chest pointed toward the two women. My omega trembles, but I shift her into a cradle hold and use a finger under her chin to guide her attention across the room.

"Coral, meet Thia and Sky, the only two females on my crew."

She stiffens and swings her gaze up to mine for a quick perusal of my face before returning her attention to the women.

"Crew, as in they help run the ship?"

Thia steps forward and gives a slight bow as she speaks.

"I'm the navigation officer on Crew B, ma'am."

"And I'm the medical officer for Crew B and every female onboard. The only omega I've ever treated is currently eight years old, but if you need anything, I'll be happy to help," Sky says.

Coral stares at them as though their words bounce off her skull, but neither female fidgets. Long, tense moments pass.

Worms crawl in my belly as my omega swings her eyes up to mine. Her shrunken pupils reveal irises so grey they appear clear.

"You mean they aren't wet nurses?"

I don't understand her question. Thia shifts and Sky rubs her nape.

"What are you asking?" I need clarification. A single tear trails down my mate's face. My stomach drops through the floor. Coral pushes against my chest and stumbles to her feet, and all I can do is stare in confusion.

"I thought you were bringing me to meet the women who would raise my children!" She stomps her bare foot and clenches her fists at her sides before stepping back and wrapping her arms around her stomach. “You can’t take my younglings away. They’re mine! I want them with me all the time. If you—”

I surge to my feet and wrap my arms around her.

“Hush, little angel. No one will separate you from our offspring,” I growl into her hair.

She thumps her fists against my sides and shakes her head. I take a deep breath, needing to settle my racing heart, and exhale on a low, soothing rumble. As my female’s madness slowly abates, I smooth my hand over her hair and murmur encouraging words in her ear, needing her to see the truth in my heart.

With one final thump of her fist against my hip, she wraps her arms around my waist and hiccups into my chest. I drop my cheek to the top of her head and return her embrace.

“No one will take your younglings from you, Coral. You haven’t seen our entire den yet, have you?”

She shakes her head.

“We have a second, smaller washroom, a kitchen, a living room, a gym, and two nurseries. And we can always expand, too. The compartment next to—”

Dainty fingers settle over my lips. My omega offers me a peek into her turmoil before closing her eyes. An odd tugging inside my chest makes me realize she's studying our bond.

She releases her breath and shakes her head. My lungs seize.

"I'm sorry, Port."

"No," I growl on instinct.

She huffs a half laugh before capturing my face between her hands. Emotions shine from her eyes as she traces the scar over my lips with her thumb.

"I'm sorry I doubted you," she whispers.

"What?"

The terror gripping my heart steals my ability to think.

"I'm sorry I lumped you in with other alphas. I'm sorry I compared you to The Sisters. I'm sorry I didn't trust you," she says, her voice strengthening with every word.

The band around my chest loosens.

"I love you, Port. Forgive me?"

My mind splinters. Relief gathers my thoughts and I suck down a breath to offer her a deep purr.

"I'll forgive you this time, but don't doubt me again, or I may rut you so hard neither of us recovers. Even the devil himself has limits, my little fallen angel," I snarl before dropping my face to hers.

I consume her mouth with the passion roaring through me, but when she rubs her thighs together and her scent thickens in the air, I snatch her off the ground and stomp toward our den.

I must please and pamper my pregnant omega. She'll require my seed day and night for the next few weeks, otherwise our offspring will consume her from the inside out.

Today marks the beginning of our future. With no misunderstandings between us, we drop into our filthy nest and explore each other anew. As we bask in our joining, our bond glows with joy and satisfaction.

This ethereal beauty is mine. Mine to cherish. Mine to hurt. Mine to love.

For years to come, she'll carry my offspring in her womb. She'll nurture our babes in her arms, smother them with her love, and give them a safe place to grow before they leave the nest to find their own way in the world.

She's the center of my universe. My purpose for living. The bearer of my future.

My angel. My omega. My Coral.

Mine.

Forever.

BRED BY THE BARGE (PREVIEW)

The Knottiverse: Alphas of the Waterworld
Book 7

CHAPTER 2

Pearl

Time distorts.

A shadow spans over my sister's face. I look up—and up—into eyes as clear and bright as the shallows. Flecks of gold and green shine from his otherwise dark face as his silhouette blocks the sun.

With broad shoulders and a towering frame, he's the largest alpha I've ever seen. Either that, or he's a god stranded in this cruel dystopian world. Or the first mountain to sprout from the depths of the ocean in centuries. Or —

My mind splinters as the behemoth leans down and proves his strength by pulling me, my sister, and the broken barrel out of the water in one smooth motion. He doesn't groan at the weight of our waterlogged clothes or hiss at the awkward tangle of limbs. He strides over a net made of thick rope as though it were a solid surface and steps onto a silvery deck. I marvel at the rust-free surface as he drops into a squat and sets us down.

For a moment, relief steals my strength. My head swims and phantom currents tug at my legs. I can't release the barrel. Can't roll off Gem. Can't breathe.

I give in to the darkness hovering along the edge of my vision, only to snap awake in panic.

Sharks. Blood. Fire. Screams.

Agony lances through my fingers as gigantic hands pry them off the barrel. Scarred knuckles fill my vision, but saving my sister is more important than protecting myself, so I shove the male away and throw myself over her in an uncoordinated heap.

"Don't touch her," I snarl. My voice doesn't sound like my own after countless hours of choking on saltwater.

Hard hands grab me and the world shifts. My head spins long after my back hits the deck, but I scramble upright, sink my nails into his leg, and hold on with every ounce of adrenaline pumping through me.

Thick fingers weave into my matted hair and yank my head back.

“Don’t touch her,” I croak through the haze of panic as I tighten my grip on him.

“Get your hands off me, little one, before I put mine on you.”

Continue reading *Bred by the Barge (The Knottiverse: Alphas of the Waterworld Book 7)* direct from V.T. Bonds’ website for an exclusive discount:

https://vtbonds.com/product/bred-by-the-barge/

***

Go to https://vtbonds.com for a complete list of books by V.T. Bonds.

For new releases, discounts, and Knotty Exclusives, subscribe to V.T. Bonds' newsletter at https://vtbonds.com/newslettersubscriber.

***

Embrace the dark, filthy side of omegaverse.

Brought to you by V.T. Bonds, The Knottiverse is a universe full of nesting, knots, morally grey alphas, and omegas who become the center of their mate's world.

Guaranteed to leave you slick, each story contains an HEA and at least one larger-than-life alpha.

Enter The Knottiverse now at:

https://vtbonds.com/the-knottiverse/

KEEP UP WITH V.T. BONDS

My Newsletter:

https://vtbonds.com/newslettersubscriber/

My website:

https://vtbonds.com/

Find me on:

Bookbub

Goodreads

Facebook

Milton Keynes UK
Ingram Content Group UK Ltd.
UKHW021015270524
443319UK00017B/827